listening

speaking

writing

All in
Reading

book two

余光雄
Grover K. H. Yu, PhD
學歷 /
美國新墨西哥大學語言教育學博士

三民書局

國家圖書館出版品預行編目資料

All in Reading book two／余光雄編著.－－初版一
刷.－－臺北市：三民，2010
　　面；　公分

ISBN 978–957–14–5266–1　（平裝）

　　1.英語 2.讀本

805.18　　　　　　　　　　　　　　　98018390

©　All in Reading book two

編 著 者	余光雄
責任編輯	陳逸如
美術設計	謝岱均

發 行 人	劉振強
著作財產權人	三民書局股份有限公司
發 行 所	三民書局股份有限公司
	地址　臺北市復興北路386號
	電話　(02)25006600
	郵撥帳號　0009998–5
門 市 部	(復北店)臺北市復興北路386號
	(重南店)臺北市重慶南路一段61號

| 出版日期 | 初版一刷　2010年1月 |
| 編 　 號 | S 809070 |

行政院新聞局登記證局版臺業字第○二○○號

有著作權‧不准侵害

ISBN　978–957–14–5266–1　（平裝）

http://www.sanmin.com.tw　三民網路書店
※本書如有缺頁、破損或裝訂錯誤，請寄回本公司更換。

序

　　「閱讀」在學習外（英）語的過程中佔極重要的角色。「閱讀」可說是最方便、最直接且最常用的英語學習途徑。因此，閱讀教材的好壞會直接影響到學習效果。坊間雖然有很多進口的英文教材，但由於不是針對技術學院學生及高職或綜合高中的學生編寫，以至於唸英文變成一種痛苦與折磨，教師在實際教學時也有不便之處。尤其在固定的進度壓力下，授課時數又有限，讓師生覺得學習英文是萬分的辛苦。

　　《All in Reading 全方位英文閱讀》這本英文讀本是在考慮上述諸問題的各層面，以及要幫助師生在課堂內能夠培養聽、說、讀、寫四種技能的需求下而編撰的。這本英文讀本的特色就是它照顧了聽、說、讀、寫四種能力的均衡發展；學生既不必為聽力練習多帶一本課本，也不必為英文寫作多帶一本課本，因為本讀本就含有這一類的學習材料。這也就是本書取名「全方位英文閱讀」的原因。

　　筆者編撰此書時，時時刻刻想到老師要如何教，學生要如何學的問題，所以本英文讀本是以課堂教學為導向、以輕鬆有趣為方針、以生活化為原則，相信定能為學習者帶來事半功倍的效益。其中若有疏漏之處，祈請方家不吝指教。

余光雄謹識

|CONTENTS|

UNIT 1
Stop the Expansion of Deserts

Warm-up

Look at the pictures below and answer the following questions.

1. How is a desert formed?
2. How do deserts affect our lives?
3. Why is it difficult to grow plants in deserts?

Reading task

Stop the Expansion of Deserts

Look at a globe or a map of the world. Find the deserts. Where are they? These dry regions, such as the Sahara, the Kalahari, the Gobi, are getting larger. They are growing fast. The expansion of dry, useless land is a serious problem. Because the number of people in the world is increasing, the need for food is also becoming greater. Crops can't grow in a desert, so people must stop the growth of deserts. The world needs more usable land, not less.

Scientists are trying to find a way to stop the expansion of arid land. They want to find ways to fight back. They are trying to understand the reasons for desert expansion.

Thus far, they have identified three reasons. The most important reason for the expansion of deserts is the climate pattern of the world. Weather systems, especially the winds, over the desert areas dry out the land. Second, there are few rivers in these regions, so there is nothing to replace the lost water. In addition, people have changed the land. Simple changes can upset the balance of nature—a desert is a fragile environment. However, people have needs. For example, people need food, and they must clear land for fields and plant crops for food. They leave the land without the protection of plants; therefore, winds can dry the land.

A third reason for the expansion of deserts is the number of animals. They provide milk and meat for people, but there are too many animals for the fragile environment of these areas. Hungry animals eat the grass, even the roots. They leave the land bare. Then the land is not protected against the dry winds.

People can't change the climate, but they can protect the land. They can plant trees and grasses. They can limit the number of animals too. People can be careful in their use of water and stop the expansion of deserts.

cactus blossom

Vocabulary Note

1. globe *n.* 地球儀
2. desert *n.* 沙漠
3. region *n.* 區域
4. crop *n.* 農作物
5. usable *adj.* 可用的
6. arid *adj.* 乾燥的
7. fight back 反抗
8. identify *v.* 確認
9. climate *n.* 氣候
10. pattern *n.* 形態
11. replace *v.* 取代
12. upset the balance of 干擾…平衡
13. fragile *adj.* 脆弱的
14. root *n.* 樹（草）根
15. bare *adj.* 光禿的；荒涼的
16. protect *v.* 保護
17. limit *v.* 限制

■ Reading Comprehension Check ■

Part A

According to the text you read, if the following statement is true, put "T" in the blank; if not, put "F" in the blank.

_____ 1. Deserts have stopped growing since last year.

_____ 2. A desert is not a fragile environment.

_____ 3. The world needs more usable land because the need for food is increasing.

_____ 4. We can't change the climate, but we can protect the land.

_____ 5. The climate pattern is not the major reason for the expansion of deserts.

_____ 6. People cut plants which are the protection of land.

_____ 7. Winds do no changes to the land.

_____ 8. The number of animals and human population can't be the reasons for the expansion of deserts.

_____ 9. People leave the land without the protection of plants and animals eat the grass on the land.

_____ 10. Without plant roots, water can't be stored in the land.

Part B

According to the text you read, answer the following questions.

( ) 1. Which of the following is the theme of the article?

　　(A) Paying attention to the climate pattern of the world.

　　(B) Stopping the growth of deserts.

　　(D) Creating more deserts.

　　(C) Finding ways to replace the lost water on Earth.

( ) 2. Which of the following statements is NOT the reason for the expansion of deserts?

　　(A) The number of animals.

　　(B) The number of deserts.

　　(C) Weather systems, especially the winds, will dry out the land.

　　(D) There is no way to replace the lost water in the deserts.

( ) 3. Why should we stop the land becoming deserts?

　　(A) There are fewer and fewer rivers in the world.

　　(B) We can't grow crops in a desert and the need for food is getting greater.

　　(C) Deserts will damage the world's weather patterns.

　　(D) We can raise animals in deserts.

( ) 4. According to the article, what do animals provide for people?

　　(A) Milk and meat.　　　　　　(B) Bread and butter.

　　(C) Salt and pepper.　　　　　(D) Sugar and spice.

( ) 5. According to the article, which of the following statements is correct?

　　(A) We can grow crops in a desert.

　　(B) We can use the climate pattern to improve the fragile environment.

　　(C) We can change the climate, but we can't protect the land.

　　(D) We have changed the land and upset the balance of nature in deserts.

■ Reading for Details

According to the text you read, select one proper word for each blank.

How can we stop the expansion of deserts? We must realize the reasons for the expansion of deserts. ¹_____ scientists have identified some reasons. One of ²_____ is the climate pattern of the world. Weather has strong influence ³_____ our lives. ⁴_____ winds for example—they have strong power to dry out the land. Many ⁵_____ areas thus become deserts after the winds dry them out.

( ) 1. (A) How far   (B) Therefore   (C) However   (D) So far

( ) 2. (A) them   (B) they   (C) themself   (D) themselves

( ) 3. (A) over   (B) with   (C) from   (D) about

( ) 4. (A) Takes   (B) Took   (C) Take   (D) Taken

( ) 5. (A) usable   (B) weak   (C) empty   (D) useless

■ Expanding Vocabulary

Part A

Match the words on the left with the definitions on the right.

1. globe	(A) the Earth
2. crop	(B) a plant grown by farmers for food
3. increase	(C) to recognize discover
4. identify	(D) to get larger in number; to add
5. climate	(E) in a steady state
6. replace	(F) empty; not covered
7. balance	(G) easily broken or damaged
8. fragile	(H) surroundings
9. environment	(I) to take the place of; to substitute
10. bare	(J) the typical weather conditions in a particular area

1. _____   2. _____   3. _____   4. _____   5. _____

6. _____   7. _____   8. _____   9. _____   10. _____

Part B

Select the best word to fill in the blank in each sentence.

( ) 1. _____ land is so dry that very few plants can grow on it.
   (A) Usable   (B) Arid   (C) Swamp   (D) Bare

( ) 2. Gina loves Anthony so much, and she thinks that no one can _____ him.
   (A) replace   (B) balance   (C) surround   (D) upset

( ) 3. Can you _____ the murderer who killed your husband?
   (A) plant   (B) replace   (C) limit   (D) identify

( ) 4. A red blanket covered Sue's _____ legs.
   (A) bare   (B) fragile   (C) arid   (D) changed

( ) 5. The humid _____ made John feel uncomfortable.
   (A) temperature (B) surrounding (C) climate   (D) custom

( ) 6. The farmer finds a good place to grow _____.
   (A) crops   (B) flops   (C) drops   (D) props

( ) 7. A(n) _____ is a large area where no water or plants can be found.
   (A) dessert   (B) island   (C) swamp   (D) desert

( ) 8. A glass window is very _____ because it can be broken easily.
   (A) expensive (B) fragile   (C) fragrant   (D) elegant

( ) 9. We traveled the _____ in order to find treasure.
   (A) globe   (B) glove   (C) glow   (D) growth

( )10. In the country, the urban population is _____.
   (A) increasing (B) fragile   (C) usable   (D) arid

Part C

Select a proper phrase to complete each of the following sentences. Make changes if necessary.

> thus far   reason for   find ways to   dry...out   protected against
> north of   in addition   careful in   need for   in addition to

1. This country has a strong _____ a high speed railway.
2. The water in the lake has to be well _____ pollution.
3. Can you give me a _____ doing this?
4. _____ providing nutrition, the bread tastes delicious.
5. No city officers have _____ solve traffic problem.
6. _____, I've told you all I knew.
7. May hung her skirt on a hook in order to _____ it _____.
8. The rich are often proud; _____ they tend to laugh at the poor.
9. Tainan is located in the _____ Kaohsiung City.
10. For happiness, you must be _____ choosing your lifelong partner.

Speaking task

Group Discussion

Discuss the following questions with your group members. Then, report your answers to the class.

1. How do we know that the deserts are spreading?
2. What would we do if there's not enough land?
3. What can we do to stop the expansion of deserts?
4. If the word becomes a desert, what will happen?

Conversation Practice

Practice the following conversation in pairs.

Mark: Hey, Anna. Where can we see deserts on Earth?

Anna: Most of them are located between 15 degrees and 30 degrees north or south of the equator.

Mark: What do we call these areas?

Anna: They are called the desert belt.

Mark: Do you know the biggest desert in the world?

Anna: The Sahara.

Mark: How big is it?

Anna: It is 9,000,000 square kilometers, almost as large as the United States.

Mark: Why do we need to protect forests?

Anna: Forests can protcet the land.

Mark: What may happen if people leave the land without the protection of plants and let the winds dry it out?

Anna: The land will become a desert and people will not have enough usable land.

Mark: Wow. Is there anything we can do to prevent it?

Anna: We can protect the land or we can be careful in our use of water.

listening task

Part A

Listen to the sentences on the CD carefully, and fill in the missing words in the blanks.

1. Scientists want to _____ _____ _____ the spread of deserts.

2. _____ can't grow in deserts, so we must stop the _____ of deserts.

3. There is nothing to _____ the lost water on the land.

4. The land is left _____, not well _____ against the winds.

5. There are too many animals for the _____ _____.

6. People can't change the _____, but they can protect the land.

7. People can be careful _____ their use of water so as to help stop the desert _____.

8. Animals _____ the land without the natural _____ of plants.

9. Simple changes can _____ the _____ of nature.

10. We need more _____ land, not _____.

 **Part B**

Listen to the CD. Select the most appropriate description for each picture.

1. _____

2. _____

3. _____

4. _____

🎵 **Part C**

Listen to the CD. According to what you hear, select the best answer to each question.

(   ) 1. What are they talking about?
      (A) The deserts.
      (B) Globe warming.
      (C) Water shortage.
      (D) Planting trees and flowers.

(   ) 2. According to the dialogue, what's the reason for the expansion of deserts?
      (A) People won't have enough useable land.
      (B) The deserts come under attack.
      (C) People need more and more dry land.
      (D) The change of the climate pattern in the world.

(   ) 3. Which desert is mentioned in the dialogue?
      (A) The Gobi.
      (B) The Arabian Desert.
      (C) The Sahara.
      (D) The Syrian Desert.

(   ) 4. What can we do to protect the environment?
      (A) We can plant trees and grasses.
      (B) We can change the climate pattern.
      (C) We can waste water.
      (D) We can leave the land without plants.

(   ) 5. What is the girl concerned about?
      (A) She is concerned about the climate in the world.
      (B) She is concerned about the plants in the world.
      (C) She is concerned about the expansion of deserts.
      (D) She is concerned about the water shortage.

Sentence Patterns

Part A

Use the given structures to translate each of the following into English.

> ● **1. A + be + (not) + as + Adj. + as + B.**

Examples:

1. Tom is as tall as his brother.

2. Kevin's house is not as big as Jack's.

Exercises:

1. Lisa跑的和Sally一樣快。

2. Bill不像他哥哥一樣強壯。

3. Susan跟她母親一樣活躍。

4. 這個麵包像籃球一樣大。

5. Jason跟Ricky一樣有錢。

2. A + be + Adj.-er + than + B.
A + be + less + Adj. + than + B.

Examples:

1. Betty is older than Kitty.
2. My car is smaller than Jim's.
3. Serena is less active than Lily.

Exercises:

1. Grace比Kenny還聰明。

2. Helen的電腦比Linda的還好。

3. 在這會議中，David 比他的伙伴還緊張。

4. Jeff比Ray還重。

5. Andy比他的老闆還忙碌。

6. 這隻手機比一本書還便宜。

UNIT 2 Communications Satellite

Warm-up

Look at the pictures below and answer the following questions.

1. What can communications satellites do in our daily life?
2. What are the advantages or disadvantages of satellite communications?

📖 Reading task

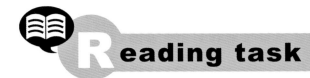

🎵 Communications Satellite

High above the Earth, there are numbers of communications **satellites**. **Rockets** take them high into the sky, usually about 22,300 miles, or 35,900 **kilometers**, above the Earth's **surface**. Like the moon, Earth's only natural satellite, communications satellites travel in a great **circle** (an **orbit**) around our **planet**. Most of these satellites travel at the same speed as the Earth, so they seem to always stay in the same place in the sky. Stations on the ground, called Earth stations, send **signals** to these satellites. The stations carry equipment to **relay** the signals. Because of these satellites, communication can be easy and **rapid**.

At the beginning, communications satellites were like "sound" or "signal" mirrors. Like a person looking in a mirror, the returning signal was a **reflection** of the original signal. Today, however, communications satellites are all active **devices**. They receive the signals, **amplify** or **strengthen** them, and then relay them.

As these satellites circle the Earth, messages are sent to them by radio waves. These radio signals travel in **straight** lines. By using a satellite to receive and then **transmit** the signals, **technicians** are sure that the messages will continue to travel. The waves travel in a straight line up to a satellite and then in a straight line down to the Earth at an **angle**.

Because there are a large number of communications satellites, a message can go up and down as many times as necessary to reach anyone anywhere on the planet. One satellite at 22,300 miles above the Earth can send signals to about one third of the planet. Therefore, with three satellites in the proper places, messages can be sent to everywhere on Earth. Communications satellites can transmit the signals **immediately**.

These satellites make it possible for an **event** in one part of the world to be seen on television everywhere at the same time. Moreover, today telephone calls between any two places on Earth are no longer a dream.

Vocabulary Note

1. satellite *n.* 衛星
2. rocket *n.* 火箭
3. kilometer *n.* 公里
4. surface *n.* 表面
5. circle *n.* 圓圈
6. orbit *n.* 軌道
7. planet *n.* 行星
8. signal *n.* 信號
9. relay *v.* 傳遞
10. rapid *adj.* 快速的
11. reflection *n.* 反射
12. device *n.* 裝置
13. amplify *v.* 擴大
14. strengthen *v.* 強化
15. straight *adj.* 直線的
16. transmit *v.* 傳送
17. technician *n.* 技術人員
18. angle *n.* 角度
19. immediately *adv.* 立即地
20. event *n.* 事件

■ Reading Comprehension Check ▬▬▬

Part A

According to the text you read, if the following statement is true, put "T" in the blank; if not, put "F" in the blank.

_____ 1. Airplanes take communications satellites high into the sky.

_____ 2. Most of these satellites around our planet seem to always stay in the same place in the sky.

_____ 3. There are several natural satellites around the Earth.

_____ 4. One satellite can send signals to about two thirds of the Earth.

_____ 5. Because of the satellites, communication between any two places on Earth are now possible.

■ Reading Comprehension Check ▬▬▬

Part B

According to the text you read, answer the following questions.

(　) 1. By what are messages sent to the Earth?

    (A) Rockets.　　(B) Radio waves.(C) Sound.　　　(D) Planes.

(　) 2. How many times can a message go up and down to the Earth?

    (A) As many times as necessary.　(B) Three times a day.

    (C) Twice a month.　　　　　　(D) Once a week.

(　) 3. How long does satellite communication take?

    (A) Twenty minutes.　　　　(B) Very slow.

    (C) Almost immediately.　　(D) Twice a week.

(　) 4. How many natural satellites does Earth have?

    (A) One.　　(B) Two.　　(C) Three .　　(D) Four.

(　) 5. At least how many satellites do we need to make messages transmit everywhere on Earth?

    (A) One.　　(B) Two.　　(C) Three.　　(D) Four.

■ Expanding Vocabulary

Part A

Select the best word to fill in the blank in each sentence.

(   ) 1. Sue is not here now. Can I take a _____ ?

      (A) light   (B) picture   (C) voice   (D) message

(   ) 2. People in Taiwan today _____ abroad more often than before.

      (A) walk   (B) travel   (C) ride   (D) invite

(   ) 3. Kelly's hair is not curly but _____ .

      (A) long   (B) round   (C) square   (D) straight

(   ) 4. It is _____ to make a monkey act like a man.

      (A) possible   (B) normal   (C) unusual   (D) different

(   ) 5. Daniel says that he wants to visit every city _____ the island.

      (A) between   (B) above   (C) about   (D) on

(   ) 6. Nancy looked at herself in a _____ .

      (A) mirror   (B) station   (C) rocket   (D) satellite

(   ) 7. The values are _____ from generation to generation.

      (A) circled   (B) bounced   (C) strengthened (D) transmitted

(   ) 8. Jogging can _____ the functions of the heart and lungs.

      (A) large   (B) strengthen   (C) power   (D) reduce

(   ) 9. It's easy for me to _____ these boxes at the same time.

      (A) fix   (B) catch   (C) carry   (D) use

(   )10. Jeff went home _____ when he heard the bad news.

      (A) rapid   (B) fast   (C) slow   (D) immediately

Part B

Give the proper form of the following words.

Noun	Verb	Adjective
1. action	act	active
2.		reflective
3. communication		
4.	strengthen	

Part C

Match the words on the left with the definitions on the right.

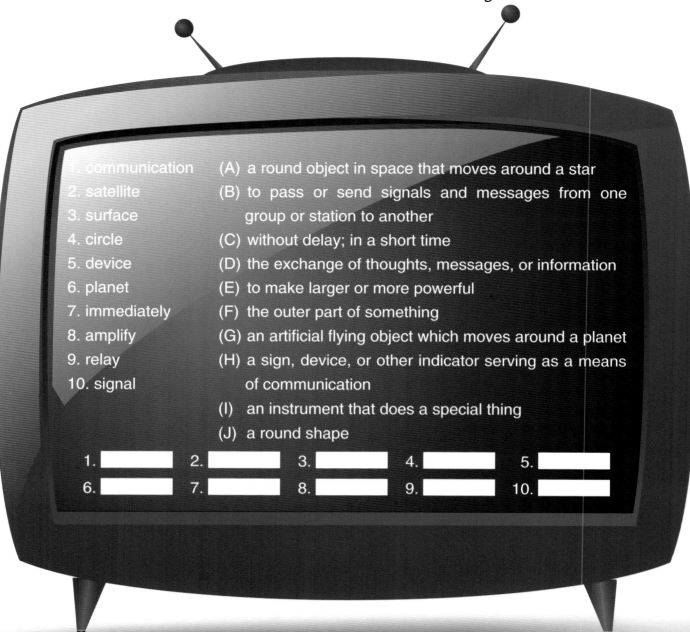

1. communication   (A) a round object in space that moves around a star

2. satellite   (B) to pass or send signals and messages from one group or station to another

3. surface

4. circle   (C) without delay; in a short time

5. device   (D) the exchange of thoughts, messages, or information

6. planet   (E) to make larger or more powerful

7. immediately   (F) the outer part of something

8. amplify   (G) an artificial flying object which moves around a planet

9. relay   (H) a sign, device, or other indicator serving as a means of communication

10. signal

(I) an instrument that does a special thing

(J) a round shape

1. ☐   2. ☐   3. ☐   4. ☐   5. ☐

6. ☐   7. ☐   8. ☐   9. ☐   10. ☐

Phrase Drill

Select a proper phrase to complete each of the following sentences. Make changes if necessary.

> so...that   as...as   up and down   more than   a large number of

1. It is _____ cold _____ we had better stay in the house.
2. There are _____ fishes in the lake, so I like to go fishing there with my friends.
3. Dan was so worried that he kept walking _____.
4. Justin can run _____ fast _____ Billy.
5. There are _____ fifty people living in the building.

Speaking task

Conversation Practice

Practice the following conversation in pairs.

Carter : Have you ever heard about communications satellites?

Rachel: No, never. What's that?

Carter : Communications satellites make it possible for an event to be seen on TV everywhere at the same time.

Rachel: Wow, I never think about that. How do you know that?

Carter : I read an article on satellites in a book.

Rachel: Any more information about the satellites?

Carter : Yes, there are several satellites being used by Asian countries now.

Rachel: No wonder we can see news immediately no matter where we are.

Carter : Besides, communications satellites can transmit signals almost instantaneously.

Rachel: Cool, can we find them in the sky?

Carter : That's impossible. They are sent high into space by rockets.

Group Discussion

Discuss the following questions with your group members, and then report your answers to the class.

1. What would we do without communications satellites?

2. How do you communicate with your friends?

 Listening task

Part A

If the sentence you hear on the CD means the same as the one below, put "S" in the blank; if not, put "D" in the blank.

_____ 1. It takes a communications satellite a long time to transmit the signals.

_____ 2. Because of the satellites, communication can be easy and rapid.

_____ 3. We use airplanes to take rockets high into the sky.

_____ 4. Stations on the ground, called mother ship, send signals to these satellites.

_____ 5. Most of these satellites travel at the same speed as the moon.

Part B

Listen to the sentences on the CD carefully, and fill in the missing words in the blanks.

1. Like a person looking in a _____ , the returning signal was a _____ of the original signal.
2. With three satellites in the _____ places, messages can be sent to _____ on Earth.
3. The waves travel at an _____ to a satellite and then in a _____ line down to the Earth.
4. _____ satellites are all active _____ .
5. The _____ of the satellites _____ the signals.

Writing task

Translation

Translate each of the following Chinese sentence into English.

1. 據說這種疾病是經由空氣傳染。
   It was said that the disease was _____ the air.

2. 為了觀察鳥巢，Frank以某種角度站著。
   Frank was standing _____ in order to watch the bird's nest.

3. Amanda看著她在水中的倒影。
   Amanda looking at her _____ the lake.

4. 煙火是撤退的信號。
   The fireworks is the _____ for the soldiers retreat.

5. 根據調查顯示，三分之一的學生都過重。
   According to the survey, _____ the students are overweight.

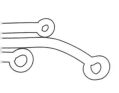

▰ Grammar Focus ▰

There are a few grammatical in the following passage. Underline the errors, and write the correct answers in the box given below the passage.

At the beginning, communications satellites are like sound or signal mirrors. Like a person looked in a mirror, the returning signal was a reflection on the original signal. Today, however, communications satellites are all active device. They receive the signals, amplify or strengthen them, and then relayed them.

Error	Correction

Culture Shock

Warm-up

Here are some pictures of people of different cultures. Math each of the following pictures with its description.

A.

B.

C.

D.

E.

(　) 1. Indian culture.

(　) 2. Western culture.

(　) 3. Jewish culture.

(　) 4. African culture.

(　) 5. Japanese culture.

Reading task

Culture Shock

Living in a new country is not always wonderful and exciting. Culture shock is the feeling that people experience when they come to a new environment. Specialists say that it is not easy to adjust to life in a new culture.

According to the specialists, there are three stages of culture shock. First, the newcomers like the environment. Then, they begin to hate the new culture when the newness disappears. Finally, they begin to adjust themselves to the environment and enjoy their lives more.

Here are some of the obvious reasons for culture shock, such as the unpleasant weather, the different customs, the public service system difficult to them and the strange food. Moreover, if you don't look similar to the natives, you may feel strange. You may feel like everyone is watching you. In fact, you are always watching yourself. You are self-conscious.

Everyone experiences culture shock in some form or another. But culture shock comes as a surprise to most people. Very often the people with the worst culture shock are the people who never had any difficulties in their own countries. When they come to a new

country, they do not have the same established positions or hobbies. They find themselves without a role, almost without an identity. They have to build a new self-image.

Culture shock produces a feeling of disorientation. When people feel the disorientation of culture shock, they sometimes feel like staying inside all the time. They want to protect themselves from the unfamiliar environment. They want to create an escape within their rooms to give themselves a sense of security. This escape does solve the problem of culture shock for the short term, but it does nothing to familiarize the person more with the culture. Familiarity and experience are the long-term solutions to the problem of culture shock.

Vocabulary Note

1. shock n. 衝擊
2. adjust v. 適應
3. stage n. 階段
4. obvious adj. 明顯的
5. self-conscious adj. 太在意別人的眼光
6. established adj. 已建立的
7. position n. 身份地位
8. identity n. 身份
9. disorientation n. 失落
10. escape n. 逃避
11. security n. 安全
12. familiarize v. 使熟悉
13. familiarity n. 熟悉
14. solution n. 解決的辦法

■ Reading Comprehension Check ▬▬▬

According to the text you read, answer the following questions.

(　　) 1. What is the main theme of the article?

    (A) It is necessary to study different cultures.

    (B) It describes what culture shock is like.

    (C) Culture shock is a sense of security.

    (D) Culture shock produces complicated disorientation.

(　　) 2. Which of the following is NOT an obvious reason for culture shock?

    (A) Unpleasant weather.   (B) Different customs.

    (C) Strange food.   (D) Friendly people.

(　　) 3. According to the article, which is the second stage of culture shock?

    (A) The newcomers like the environment.

    (B) The newcomers feel excited and happy.

    (C) The newcomers look similar to the natives.

    (D) The newcomers hate the new culture when the newness disappears.

(　　) 4. What is the solution to the problem of culture shock?

    (A) Familiarity and experience.   (B) Yell and scream.

    (C) Escape and hide.   (D) Wait and see.

(　　) 5. When people feel the disorientation of culture shock, what might they do?

    (A) They often make all kinds of mistakes.

    (B) They feel like staying inside all the time.

    (C) They don't want to protect themselves.

    (D) They don't want to enjoy their lives.

(　　) 6. Culture shock is _____.

    (A) the feeling that we experience when we come to a new country

    (B) a social problem that might cause accident

    (C) a nightmare some people may have when they fall asleep

    (D) an economic problem which newcomers can't get used to

(   ) 7. You may feel like everyone is watching you because _____.

    (A) you are so attractive

    (B) the weather is unpleasant

    (C) you are always watching yourself

    (D) you don't like the people at all

(   ) 8. What kind of people may have the worst culture shock?

    (A) Those who don't like other cultures.

    (B) Those who are young and less experienced.

    (C) Those who don't have cultural background.

    (D) Those who never had any difficulties in their own countries.

(   ) 9. Which of the following is produced by culture shocks?

    (A) A feeling of disorientation.   (B) A feeling of happiness.

    (C) A sense of security.   (D) A sense of humor.

(   ) 10. How do people who experience culture shock behave?

    (A) They learn several foreign languages.

    (B) They change their hairstyle.

    (C) They go to a doctor.

    (D) They create an escape so as to achieve a sense of security.

■ Reading for Details

According to the text you read, select one proper word for each blank.

According to the specialists, there are three stages of culture shock. First, the newcomers like the environment. [1]_____, they begin to hate the new culture when the [2]_____ disappears. Finally, they begin to [3]_____ themselves to the environment and enjoy their lives more.

Everyone [4]_____ culture shock in some form or another. But culture shock comes [5]_____ a surprise to most people. Most of the time, the people [6]_____ the worst culture shock are the people who never had any difficulties [7]_____ their own countries. [8]_____ they come to a new country, they don't have the same established positions or hobbies. They find themselves without a [9]_____, even without an identity. When they feel the disorientation of culture shock, they sometimes feel like [10]_____ inside all the time. They want to protect themselves from the unfamiliar environment.

(   )   1. (A) So   (B) Then   (C) What   (D) Early

(   )   2. (A) happiness   (B) carelessness (C) newness   (D) loneliness

(   )   3. (A) adopt   (B) adapt   (C) adjust   (D) accord

(   )   4. (A) changes   (B) creates   (C) develops   (D) experiences

(   )   5. (A) as   (B) to   (C) in   (D) on

(   )   6. (A) with   (B) from   (C) by   (D) of

(   )   7. (A) from   (B) with   (C) in   (D) of

(   )   8. (A) How   (B) Where   (C) What   (D) When

(   )   9. (A) ring   (B) role   (C) road   (D) room

(   ) 10. (A) stayed   (B) stays   (C) staying   (D) stay

▪ Expanding Vocabulary

In this part you will learn two ways to derive a new word from the given word. Give the negative prefix to each of the following words. Make changes if necessary.

Prefix "dis-"

Add the prefix "dis-" to the beginning of the word.

(1) appear → **dis**appear

(2) advantage → _____   (3) agree → _____

(4) approve → _____   (5) honest → _____

Prefix "un-"

Add the prefix "un-" to the beginning of the word.

(1) happy → **un**happy

(2) fortunate → _____   (3) conscious → _____

(4) comfortable → _____   (5) lucky → _____

Speaking task

Conversation Practice

Invite a partner to practice the following conversation.

Steve : Hi, Mandy. You look so upset. Are you okay?

Mandy: I don't know. Maybe it's the weather.

Steve : Do you mean the weather is unpleasant?

Mandy: Yes. I think so. I am not accustomed to the weather here.

Steve : Here, in winter, the temperature often drops below zero.

Mandy: No wonder I always feel so cold.

Steve : What else bothers you?

Mandy: Hmm, the food.

Steve : What's the matter with the food?

Mandy: The food is cold! I am not used to it.

Steve : Don't worry about it. I had had the same problem at first. But I am OK now.

Mandy: Do I need to see a doctor?

Steve : No. You are experiencing culture shock. Once you adjust yourself well, you will be fine.

Mandy: Thank you.

Group Discussion

Form groups of four and discuss the following questions. Report your answers to the class.

1. Do people who experience culture shock have to go to a doctor? Why or why not?

2. What suggestions you may give to those who experience culture shock?

3. Do you have any experience of culture shock?

4. How do people react to culture shock?

istening task

Part A

Listen to the CD. According to what you hear, select the best answer to each question.

( ) 1. What problem does Andy have?
 (A) He has no friends.
 (B) He can't speak English fluently.
 (C) He is experiencing culture shock.
 (D) He don't know how to get along with the natives.

( ) 2. Which of the following is NOT the symptom of culture shock?
 (A) Feeling lonely. (B) Losing appetite.
 (C) Feeling homesick. (D) Feeling comfortable.

( ) 3. According to the dialogue, which of the following is correct?
 (A) All Andy needs is money.
 (B) Andy never talked to his roommate.
 (C) Andy missed his family and old friends.
 (D) Andy learned nothing from his roommate.

( ) 4. According to the dialogue, how long dose Andy have been in the U.S.?
 (A) Two years. (B) Two months. (C) Two weeks. (D) Two days.

( ) 5. How many suggestions dose Tina give Andy?
 (A) Three. (B) Four. (C) Five. (D) Six.

Part B

Listen to the sentences on the CD carefully, and fill in the missing words in the blanks.

1. Living in a new country is not always   one thinks.
2. Newcomers may find themselves without an   in a foreign country.
3. A feeling of   is caused by culture shock.
4.   and experience are the long-term to the problem of culture shock.
5. People would like to create an   within their rooms to give themselves a sense of   .

Writing task

Grammar Focus

Part A

There are several grammatical errors in each sentence below. Correct them and rewrite the sentences.

1. The reason why people experiences culture shock is that they wants to protect themselves of the unfamiliar environment.

2. The people with the worst culture shock is the people whose never had any difficulty in their own countries.

3. Newcomers begin to hated the new culture when the newness disappear.

4. You may feel like everyone are watch you.

5. According to the specialists, there are three stage for culture shock.

■ Sentence Scrambling

Re-arrange the given words to make meaningful sentences.

1. of disorientation/ culture shock/ a feeling/ produces

2. with the worst/ are/ the people/ had any difficulties/ the people/ who never/ in/ culture shock/ their own countries

3. the long-term/ familiarity/ culture shock/ and experience/ are/ solutions to/ the problem of

4. culture shock/ or another/ everyone/ in some form/ experiences

5. is not/ and exciting/ living/ always/ in/ wonderful/ a new country

■ Translation

Translate each of the following Chinese sentences into English.

1. 黑暗製造出一種不安全的感覺。

   Darkness _____ a _____ insecurity.

2. 要適應新國家的生活並不容易。

   It is not easy to _____ life in a new country.

3. Eric提供一個解決問題的辦法。

   Eric provides a _____ the problem.

4. 他們想要保護森林免於被摧毀。

   They want to _____ the forest _____ being destroyed.

5. Hank發現自己無處可去。

   Hank found _____ a place to stay.

6. Martin必須使自己熟悉這個新城市。

   Martin have to _____ himself _____ the new city.

■ Paragraph Writing

According to the question below, write a paragraph of 80 words in length to give your opinions on culture shock.

Do you think culture shock is a good (or bad) experience? When you are experiencing culture shock, what would you do?

Procrastination

Warm-up

Look at the pictures below and answer the following questions.

1. What are the disadvantages of being a procrastinator? List at least five of them.
2. If you are in a habit of procrastination, what will you do to overcome it?

Procrastination

The verb procrastinate comes from the Latin "procrastinare," which means "to postpone until tomorrow." Procrastinating is delaying doing something at a later time. Procrastinators are always putting off what they should be doing right now.

Those of us who have a tendency towards procrastination know that it is a terrible habit. Every day, we tell ourselves to start doing things immediately; however, we procrastinate our work, miss deadlines, and break promises. Because of procrastination, we are always trying to catch up. We are always doing yesterday's jobs today, and today's jobs tomorrow.

Vocabulary Note

1. procrastinate *v.* 延遲
2. postpone *v.* 拖延
3. delay *v.* 耽擱
4. put off 拖延
5. tendency *n.* 傾向；趨勢
6. deadline *n.* 截止日期

There are people who rarely procrastinate. They are highly efficient and well-organized people. They seem to get everything done on time. I suspect that they never leave home in the morning before they make the bed, never go to sleep at night before they finish their work, and are never late for appointments. As a result, they are probably always one step ahead of other people, especially those who like to procrastinate.

Maybe the way to overcome procrastination is to change ourselves gradually. We can start with a daily schedule of the things we need to accomplish. But let's be reasonable. We shouldn't have a busy schedule. We should be realistic about what we can do. Especially in the beginning, we should be lenient with ourselves. After all, if we fail at the start, we will get discouraged and go right back to our old habits.

7. **rarely** *adv.* 很少

8. **efficient** *adj.* 有效率的

9. **organized** *adj.* 有條理的

10. **suspect** *v.* 懷疑；猜想

11. **make bed** *v.* 鋪床

12. **schedule** *n.* 進度表；行程表

13. **reasonable** *adj.* 合理的

14. **lenient** *adj.* 寬容的

15. **discouraged** *adj.* 洩氣的

■ Reading Comprehension Check ▬▬▬▬

Part A

According to the text, select the best answer to the questions.

(   ) 1. What does the word "procrastinate"mean?

(A) To draw a plan well.   (B) To do things in advance.

(C) To postpone something.   (D) To finish work completely.

(   ) 2. Where does the word "procrastinate"come from?

(A) Greek.   (B) Latin.   (C) Chinese.   (D) Japanese.

(   ) 3. A procrastinator is one who _____.

(A) asks for others' help

(B) plans things in advance

(C) does his or her job incompletely

(D) delays doing things at a later time

(   ) 4. Which of the following is a possible way to overcome procrastination?

(A) To change it gradually.   (B) To change it rapidly.

(C) To give it up right away.   (D) To ignore it completely.

(   ) 5. If we fail at the start to overcome the habit of procrastination, we will _____.

(A) be very happy and joyful

(B) try again and won't care about the failure

(C) neglect it and be confident of success

(D) get discouraged and go right back to the old habit

Part B

According to the text you read, if the following statement is true, put "T" in the blank; if not, put "F" in the blank.

_____ 1. The verb "procrastinate" comes from the French "procrastinare," which means "hurry up."

_____ 2. A well-organized person seldom late for appointments.

_____ 3. The author advises those who want to overcome procrastination to start with a busy schedule.

_____ 4. People who rarely procrastinate are probably always one step ahead of you and me.

_____ 5. According to the article, when we make plans to break bad habits, we should be lenient ourselves in the beginning.

■ Expanding Vocabulary

Part A

Select the best word to fill the blank in each sentence.

(   ) 1. If it rains, the outdoor concert must be _____.

  (A) put off (B) turned down (C) called upon (D) switched on

(   ) 2. It took Mary a long time to _____ with her classmates.

  (A) catch up (B) brush up (C) show up (D) cover up

(   ) 3. If we miss the first bus, we can't get there _____.

  (A) out of time   (B) from time to time

  (C) on time   (D) over time

(   ) 4. Oscar was late _____ the traffic jam.

  (A) by means of   (B) due to

  (C) seem to   (D) in the event of

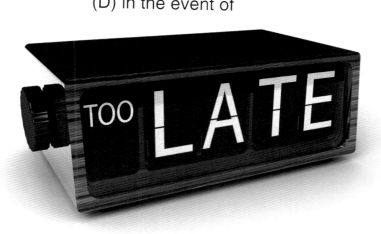

( ) 5. James never paid much attention to the teacher in the class.
_____ , he failed the exam.
    (A) As a result   (B) On the other hand
    (C) From now on   (D) At the beginning

( ) 6. We _____ Jason to know the secret.
    (A) postpone   (B) delay   (C) break   (D) suspect

( ) 7. Because we always procrastinate, we are always trying to

_____ .
    (A) wake up   (B) catch up   (C) keep out   (D) go out

( ) 8. The party _____ a fireworks display.
    (A) started with (B) skipped over (C) leaked out   (D) left alone

( ) 9. Peggy went to the school _____ us in the morning.
    (A) late for   (B) early on   (C) ahead of   (D) lenient with

( ) 10. You ought not to _____ .
    (A) break promises   (B) keep your words
    (C) fulfill promises   (D) keep promises

Part B

Match the words on the left with the definitions on the right.

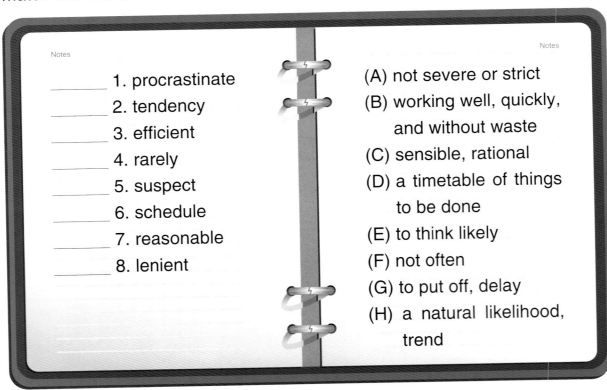

Notes

_____ 1. procrastinate
_____ 2. tendency
_____ 3. efficient
_____ 4. rarely
_____ 5. suspect
_____ 6. schedule
_____ 7. reasonable
_____ 8. lenient

Notes

(A) not severe or strict
(B) working well, quickly, and without waste
(C) sensible, rational
(D) a timetable of things to be done
(E) to think likely
(F) not often
(G) to put off, delay
(H) a natural likelihood, trend

Part C

Fill in one proper word in each blank. Make changes if necessary.

| reasonable | organized | tendency | schedule | rarely | delay |

1. It seems quite nature that the elders have a _____ to live in the past.
2. Try to be _____ . How can I give you 20 dollars when I only have 5 dollars?
3. Miracles _____ happen.
4. The teacher has a very tight _____ . She is very busy.
5. The ideas are _____ well in this report.
6. The bus was _____ because of the heavy rain.

■ Phrase Drill

Select a proper phrase to complete each of the following sentences. Make changes if necessary.

| seem to | come from | put off |
| catch up | on time | realistic about |

1. If you don't finish your work today, you have to _____ tomorrow.
2. Don't _____ what you can do today till tomorrow.
3. Rita must be _____ her power and ability.
4. If you are _____ , you are not late.
5. Do you know where this passage _____ ?
6. Rufus doesn't _____ like his daughter's boyfriend.

peaking task

◎ ▪ Conversation Practice ▬▬▬▬▬

Invite a partner to practice the following conversation.

David: Can you help me with my homework?

Betty : What? It's already ten o'clock! Why didn't you do it earlier?

David: I just couldn't. I've been working on other assignments all day long.

Betty : But you should have told me earlier. Now, I am going to bed.

David: Oh. No! Please help me! If I don't hand it in on time, I will be punished by my teacher.

Betty : You deserve it. You always repeat the same mistake. I have told you thousands of times, "Never put off until tomorrow what you can do today." It's time for you to learn a lesson and break such a terrible habit.

David: Oh, please.

Betty : Good night!

▪ Group Discussion ▬▬▬▬▬

Form groups of four and discuss the following questions. Report your answers to the class.

1. How do you manage your time?
2. What should be taken into consideration when making a reasonable schedule?
3. Have you ever missed the deadline for handing in your homework? Why?

■ Questionnaire

Make an interview with one or two of your classmates and fill out the following form.

1. Sex: _____ (Male or Female)

2. Age: _____

3. Career: _____

4. Marital status: _____ (Single or Married)

5. Do you always miss the deadline for your homework?
   - ☐ Yes.
   - ☐ No.

6. Do you often have a busy schedule?
   - ☐ Yes, always.
   - ☐ Yes, sometimes.
   - ☐ No, seldom.
   - ☐ No, never.

7. What do you think of your daily schedule?
   - ☐ Very reasonable.
   - ☐ Sort of reasonable.
   - ☐ Not reasonable.
   - ☐ Awfully tight.

8. Do you like working with a procrastinator?
   - ☐ Yes.
   - ☐ No.

9. Do you go to bed before you finish your homework?
   - ☐ Yes, always.
   - ☐ Yes, sometimes.
   - ☐ No, seldom.
   - ☐ No, never.

istening task

Part A

If the two sentences on the CD you hear mean the same, put "S" in the blank; if not, put "D" in the blank.

1. _____ 2. _____ 3. _____ 4. _____ 5. _____

Part B

If the sentence you hear on the CD means the same as the one below, put "S" in the blank; if not, put "D" in the blank.

_____ 1. A procrastinator always delays doing something at a later time.

_____ 2. The way to overcome procrastination is to change ourselves gradually.

_____ 3. We shouldn't have a busy schedule.

_____ 4. They are highly efficient and well-organized.

_____ 5. It is a good habit to put off what we should be doing right now.

riting task

■ Error Correction

Look at the passage below. There are six marked words or phrases. If the marked word or phrase is correct, put "C" in the blank. If not, put correct form in the blank.

To procrastinate is to delay doing something <u>at</u> a later time. A
                   (A)

procrastinator will always <u>putting off</u> what they should be doing right now till
               (B)

tomorrow. <u>Procrastination</u> is a terrible habit. Every day, procrastinator
         (C)

<u>ourselves</u> that they must <u>started</u> doing things right away. However, every
   (D)   (E)

day, they postpone <u>our works</u>, miss deadlines, and break promises. They
            (F)

are always doing yesterday's jobs today, and today's jobs tomorrow.

(A) _____   (B) _____   (C) _____

(D) _____   (E) _____   (F) _____

Sentence Completion

1. 汽車共乘是一個有效的節能方法。
   Car-pooling is an ______________ of saving energy.
2. 這場比賽因雨的關係延期到週五下午。
   The game was ______________ Friday afternoon because of the rain.
3. 你對你的孩子太寬容了，你在溺愛他們。
   You are ______________ your children. You are spoiling them.
4. 我們必須努力工作，不然我們會錯過截止日期。
   We have to work hard or we will ______________.
5. Maria是個無可救藥的拖延者。她從來沒有準時把功課做好。
   Maria is a hopeless ______________. She never finished her homework ______________.
6. 也許克服這個問題的方法是改變我們的生活方式。
   Maybe the way ______________ the problem is to change our lifestyle.
7. 這失敗讓Ben感到洩氣。
   This failure makes Ben feel ______________.
8. 有拖延習慣的人很容易失去成功的良機。
   People who are in the ______________ procrastination are easy to lose the opportunity to succeed.

■ Paragraph Writing

Write a paragraph of 120 words in length to give your opinions of being a procrastinator.

UNIT 5

How Much Exercise Do We Really Need?

Warm-up

Look at the pictures below and answer the following questions.

1. How much exercise do we really need?
2. What's your favorite sport?

Reading task

How Much Exercise Do We Really Need?

Ellen and David are committed to their workouts at the health club. They both go to the club every day after work and spend at least one hour doing vigorous exercise, alternating tough aerobics classes with working out on the machines and lifting weights. Both are in shape and feel fit. They believe in the motto, "No pain, no gain."

Andy and Pam are sitting in front of the television and watching yet another commercial for the local gym. It all seems overwhelming—going to the gym, working up a sweat, and even finding the time. Neither one is an athlete, nor do they really care to learn a sport now.

Are you more like Ellen and David or Andy and Pam? Or do you fall somewhere in between? We all know that exercise can help us to keep our body healthy and reduce the risks of disease. It also reduces the stress and protects the body's immune system. But for many people, the word "exercise" conjures up hours of boring, strenuous activity. Recently, however, scientific studies have found that health benefits can be achieved with non-strenuous exercise.

This is very encouraging news for all those people who thought they had to work as hard as athletes to make exercise worth it. The new guidelines say that every adult should do at least 30 minutes of moderate activity most days of the week. And these 30 minutes can even be broken down into smaller segments during the day. The important thing is to be consistent and make exercise part of your daily life.

There are many ways to achieve this without buying expensive equipment or joining a health club. For example, walking is one of the best ways to get exercise. Try to go for a walk after lunch or dinner to boost your metabolism and work off some calories. If possible, walk all or part of the way to work or school. Use the stairs instead of the elevator whenever you can. Gardening, raking leaves, and dancing are also good activities. As for sports, even if tennis or golf doesn't appeal to you, hiking and cycling can be relaxing and beneficial, too.

Remember, you can be serious about exercise without taking it too seriously!

Vocabulary Note

1. commit *v.* 投入於⋯
2. workout *n.* 健身
3. vigorous *adj.* 劇烈的
4. alternate *v.* 輪流
5. aerobics *n.* 有氧運動
6. motto *n.* 箴言
7. commercial *n.* 商業廣告
8. overwhelming *adj.*
    無法抵抗的
9. athlete *n.* 運動員
10. immune system　免疫系統
11. conjure up...　使人想起⋯

12. strenuous *adj.* 費勁的
13. benefit *n.* 益處；利益
14. guideline *n.* 指導方針
15. moderate *adj.* 適度的
16. be broken down into...
    被分成⋯
17. segment *n.* 部分
18. metabolism *n.* 新陳代謝
19. work off　消耗
20. appeal to　吸引
21. be serious about...
    對⋯認真

■Reading Comprehension Check ▬▬▬▬

Part A

According to the text you read, if the following statement is true, put "T" in the blank; if not, put "F" in the blank.

_____ 1. Andy and Pam are committed to their workouts at the health club.

_____ 2. Scientific studies have found that health benefits can be achieved with non-strenuous exercise.

_____ 3. Exercise is not important for health. It increases the risks of disease.

_____ 4. Every adult should do at least 30 minutes of moderate activity most days of the week.

_____ 5. Walking is one of the best ways to get exercise.

_____ 6. Buying expensive equipment is the best way to get exercise.

_____ 7. Exercises can reduce stress and improve our health.

_____ 8. Only athletes can do exercises.

_____ 9. We can't take exercise without joining a health club.

_____ 10. We should use the elevator instead of the stairs whenever we can.

Part B

According to the text you read, answer the following questions.

( ) 1. According to the article, what kind of sports can be relaxing and beneficial?

(A) Hiking.　　(B) Shopping.　(C) Talking.　　(D) Singing.

( ) 2. Which of the following mottos do Ellen and David believe?

(A) No pain, no gain.

(B) Where there is a will, there is a way.

(C) An eye for an eye, and we all go blind.

(D) Reading is to the mind what exercise is to the body.

( ) 3. How much time do adults need to exercise every day?

(A) 10 minutes.　(B) 30 minutes .　(C) 50 minutes.　(D) 70 minutes.

( ) 4. What can help you stay healthy and protect your body's immune system?

(A) Fooling around with friends.

(B) Drinking a lot of wine in a pub.

(C) Walking to work or school.

(D) Playing online games all night long.

( ) 5. For what purpose do people go for a walk after lunch or dinner?

(A) Appreciate the beautiful sight.

(B) In order to work off some calories.

(C) Meet some new friends on the street.

(D) Remember what happened during the day.

■Expanding Vocabulary

Part A

Match the words on the left with the definitions on the right.

_____ 1. motto

_____ 2. conjure

_____ 3. metabolism

_____ 4. strenuous

_____ 5. athlete

_____ 6. vigorous

_____ 7. commercial

_____ 8. benefit

_____ 9. moderate

_____ 10. commit

(A) one who practices physical exercises and games that need strength and speed

(B) strong, forceful

(C) an advantage

(D) to bring into mind

(E) a sentence or a few words taken as the principle of a person

(F) neither large nor small, high nor low, fast nor slow, etc.

(G) the chemical activities in a living thing by which it gains power, especially from good

(H) requiring great effort

(I) to promise (oneself, one's property, etc.) to a certain course of action

(J) an advertisement on television or radio

Part B

Choose the best answer to complete each sentence. Make changes if necessary.

| protect | achieve | encourage | equipment | beneficial |

1. My brother decided to buy new computer _____.
2. Holding an umbrella can _____ you from the sun on a sunny day.
3. In order to _____ her goal, Kate worked hard.
4. Recycling is highly _____ to the environment.
5. Steve was _____ by his teacher to become a doctor.

Part C

Select the best answer to fill in each blank.

(   ) 1. Give your upper body a _____ by using dumbbells.
    (A) printout   (B) handout   (C) workout   (D) dropout

(   ) 2. _____ exercise can increase the risk of heart attack.
    (A) Vigorous   (B) Moderate   (C) Generous   (D) Overweight

(   ) 3. My life _____ between work and sleep.
    (A) commits   (B) discharges   (C) originates   (D) alternates

(   ) 4. I'd like to join a(n) _____ class to improve my fitness.
    (A) aerobics   (B) history   (C) reading   (D) art

(   ) 5. My _____ is "Never give up."
    (A) memo   (B) motto   (C) menu   (D) motor

(   ) 6. Loker made _____ efforts to win the game.
    (A) moderate   (B) nervous   (C) strenuous   (D) dull

(　) 7. She doesn't get any _____ from this course.

    (A) owners　　(B) workouts　　(C) benefits　　(D) credits

(　) 8. The _____ won two gold medals in the Olympics.

    (A) judge　　(B) ethics　　(C) sport　　(D) athlete

(　) 9. The government has issued the _____ on the content of elementary education.

    (A) mission　　(B) admission　　(C) headlines　　(D) guidelines

(　) 10. This policy will affect large _____ of the population in the country.

    (A) segments　(B) parliaments　(C) elements　　(D) treatments

(　) 11. Ellen and David are _____ their workouts at the health club.

    (A) given to　　(B) broken into　(C) committed to (D) limited to

(　) 12. Andy and Pam are sitting _____ the television and watching yet another commercial for the local gym.

    (A) in the middle of　　　　　(B) in the front of

    (C) in front of　　　　　　　(D) in back of

(　) 13. Use the stairs _____ the elevator whenever you can.

    (A) take place　(B) instead of　　(C) substitute for (D) be replaced

(　) 14. As for sports, _____ tennis or golf doesn't attract you, hiking and cycling can be relaxing and beneficial, too.

    (A) even up　　(B) even so　　(C) even if　　(D) and even

(　) 15. Remember, you can _____ exercise without taking it too seriously.

    (A) be neglected about　　　(B) take easy to

    (C) disregard about　　　　　(D) be serious about

(　) 16. We should do _____ 30 minutes of moderate activity most days of the week.

    (A) at last　　(B) at least　　(C) at large　　(D) at all

Speaking task

■ Conversation Practice

Invite a partner to practice the following conversation.

Sherry: Hey, Brian.

Brian : Hi, Sherry.

Sherry: Wow, you look so great. What happened?

Brian : Well, I'm committed to workouts at a health club everyday.

Sherry: I see, and that's why you lose so much weight. In fact, I also want to lose some weight. I am on a diet now.

Brian : You should do some exercise. It is the best way to lose weight and it helps to achieve health benefits, too.

Sherry: I know, but for me the word "exercise" conjures up hours of boring, strenuous activities.

Brian : It's not like that. Health benefits can be achieved with non-strenuous exercise. You may go for a walk after lunch to boost your metabolism, or use the stairs instead of the elevator to work off calories.

Sherry: That sounds great. Maybe I should give it a try. I hope next time when you see me, you won't see my spare tires.

■ Role Play

Find a partner to act out the following conversation.

A: Welcome to our club. May I help you?

B: Yes, I want to lose weight. What classes should I take?

A: You can take aerobics classes.

B: How much should I pay for the classes and when can I start?

A: It's NT$10,000 dollars a year. And you can start tomorrow.

B: OK. What should I bring with me tomorrow?

A: You should bring your sportswear.

B: OK. I will start my class tomorrow. See you tomorrow.

A: See you.

Listening task

Part A

If the sentence you hear on the CD means the same as the sentence you read below, put "S" in the blank; if not, put "D" in the blank.

_____ 1. Taking exercise can damage our health.

_____ 2. Health benefits can be achieved with non-strenuous exercise.

_____ 3. You may walk all or part of the way to work as often as you can.

_____ 4. This is very encouraging news for all those people.

_____ 5. It takes them an hour to do vigorous exercise every day.

Part B

You will hear five statements on the CD. Each statement is followed by a question. According to what you hear, select the best answers to the questions.

(　) 1. (A) Bring her fame and fortune.　(B) It keeps her warm and dry.

　　　(C) Show her respect and love.　(D) Stay fit and healthy.

(　) 2. (A) Go swimming.　　　　　(B) Go hiking.

　　　(C) Attend a yoga class.　　(D) All of the above.

(　) 3. (A) Gardening.　(B) Walking.　(C) Shopping.　(D) Working.

(　) 4. (A) Cycling.　(B) Jogging.　(C) Skating.　(D) Mountaineering.

(　) 5. (A) She does nothing but cleaning the house.

　　　(B) She goes shopping when she has free time.

　　　(C) She always cooking when she has free time.

　　　(D) She does some gardening when she has free time.

■ Sentence Patterns

Use the given structure to translate each of the following into English.

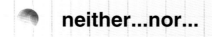

neither...nor...

Examples:

1. Neither the cat nor the dog has been fed.

2. Neither Tom nor David is an athlete.

Exercises:

Translate the following Chinese sentences into English ones.

1. Lily跟Dora昨天都沒去學校。

2. Vivian和她哥哥都不喜歡這本書。

3. Bill跟Frank都不是老師。

4. 我母親既不喝酒也不喝果汁。

5. Jenny和Monica都不是我的朋友。

■Sentence Completion ■

1. Owen每天至少花2小時看電視。

   Owen _____ at least two hours _____ TV every day.

2. 天下沒有白吃的午餐（不勞則無獲）。

   No _____, no _____.

3. Ricky跑的跟他哥哥一樣快。

   Ricky can run _____ his brother.

4. Lisa沒有告知她姐姐就去了海邊。

   Lisa went to the beach _____ her sister.

5. Adam似乎知道這個秘密。

   _____ Adam knows the secret.

■Error Correction ■

Look at the passage below. There are nine marked words or phrases. If the marked word or phrase is correct, put "C" in the blank. If not, put correct form in the blank.

There are many ways to achieve this without buy expensive equipment or
          (A)
join a health club. Walk is one of the best way to get exercise. Try to go for
(B)   (C)   (D)
a walk after lunch or dinner for boosting your metabolism and work of some
(E)   (F)   (G)
calories. If possible, walk all or part of the way to work or school. As for
         (H)
sports, even that tennis or golf doesn't appeal to you, hiking and cycling can
    (I)
be relaxing and beneficial, too.

(A) _____   (B) _____   (C) _____

(D) _____   (E) _____   (F) _____

(G) _____   (H) _____   (I) _____

■ Paragraph Writing

According to the question below, write a paragraph of 80 words in length to give your opinions on doing exercise.

What is your favorite sport? Give three reasons why you particularly like it.

Fashions

Warm-up

Look at the pictures below. Choose a correct answer for each of them and answer the questions.

1.

( )

2.

( )

3.

( )

4.

( )

5.

( )

6.

( )

A. Fedora hat.

D. Watch.

B. Sunglasses.

E. Scarf.

C. Handbag.

F. High-heeled shoes.

1. What's your favorite fashion accessory? Why?

Reading task

 Fashions

Spring, summer, fall, winter: every season, there are new clothes and new fashions in the shops. Colors and styles keep changing. One season, black is the "in" color, but the next season everyone is wearing orange or pink. One season, tight-fitting clothes are fashionable, and the next season baggy clothes are "in."

The length of women's skirts goes up and down from year to year. In the 1960s, miniskirts became very fashionable and a woman could wear a skirt twenty or thirty centimeters above the knees. A few years later, maxiskirts became trendy and then women had to wear skirts twenty or thirty centimeters below the knees. Each season there is always a "correct" length and if a woman's skirt is just a little too long or too short, some people will think that she is very unfashionable.

Vocabulary Note

1. fashion n. 流行式樣
2. style n. 流行式樣；款式
3. tight-fitting adj. 緊身的
4. fashionable adj. 流行的；時髦的
5. baggy adj. 寬鬆的
6. centimeter n. 公分
7. trendy adj. 時髦的；流行的
8. collar n. 衣領

Men also have similar problems with their shirts. Some years, it is fashionable to wear a shirt with a very small collar. Another year, small collar become outdated and large button-down collars are trendy. Sometimes it even becomes fashionable to wear shirts with no collars at all. A shirt that you once thought was very trendy can look strangely old-fashioned a few years later. And your father's shirts, which you always thought were very conservative and traditional, can suddenly seem very stylish.

Keeping up with the fashions can be very expensive. So one way to save money is keeping your old clothes. If you wait long enough, the clothes that are out of fashion today will be back in fashion tomorrow.

9. outdated *adj.* 舊式的；過時的

10. old-fashioned *adj.* 過時的

11. conservative *adj.* 舊式的

12. traditional *adj.* 傳統的

13. stylish *adj.* 時髦的；流行的

14. keep up with 跟上⋯

15. out of fashion 不合時尚的

16. in fashion 正在流行

■ Reading Comprehension Check ■

Part A

According to the text you read, if the statement is true, circle "T"; if not, circle "F."

T F 1. New fashions come out every season.

T F 2. Miniskirts are always in fashion.

T F 3. The fashionable length of a woman's skirt depends on the woman's height.

T F 4. It's a good idea to keep your parents' old clothes because they are conservative.

T F 5. The best way to save money is buying new clothes.

T F 6. Old clothes will be back in fashion someday.

Part B

According to the text you read, answer the following questions.

(   ) 1. What does the article mainly talk about?
   (A) The changing fashions.   (B) The history of miniskirts.
   (C) How to save your money.   (D) Different life style.

(   ) 2. You can tell if a woman's skirt is in fashion by its _____.
   (A) designer   (B) length   (C) button   (D) collar

(   ) 3. What kind of shirt is fashionable?
   (A) Shirts with small collars.
   (B) Shirts with button-down collars.
   (C) It depends on the trend in fashion.
   (D) Shirts with no collars.

(   ) 4. The best way to keep in fashion without spending too much money is _____.
   (A) buying all kinds of clothes at one time
   (B) always wearing the old-fashioned clothes
   (C) throwing your old clothes away
   (D) keeping your old clothes

(　　) 5. According to the article, baggy clothes are _____.

    (A) always in fashion   (B) sometimes unfashionable

    (C) always conservative   (D) seldom outdated

(　　) 6. The skirt that was _____ the knees was fashionable in the 1960s.

    (A) ten centimeters above   (B) ten centimeters below

    (C) twenty centimeters above   (D) thirty centimeters below

(　　) 7. What kind of the clothing style is called outdated?

    (A) Tight-fitting clothes.   (B) Traditional skirts.

    (C) Orange or pink clothes.   (D) It depends.

(　　) 8. This season black and gray are the _____ colors, so everybody is wearing black or gray.

    (A) on   (B) with   (C) in   (D) above

■Expanding Vocabulary

Part A

Match the words on the left with the definitions on the right.

_____ 1. baggy

_____ 2. trendy

_____ 3. conservative

_____ 4. centimeter

_____ 5. outdated

_____ 6. fashion

_____ 7. tight-fitting

_____ 8. collar

(A) not fashionable, or no longer in general use

(B) a unit of length measure

(C) loose, not tight

(D) fit closely or tightly to the body

(E) the part of a shirt that fits around the neck

(F) the way of dressing that is considered the best at a certain time

(G) fashionable

(H) unwilling to accept new ideas or any changes

Part B

In this part you will learn a way to derive a new word from the given word. Give the noun form for each of the following words. Make changes if necessary.

> **Suffix "-tion"**
>
> Add the suffix "-tion" to the end of a verb to form a noun.
>
> (1) correct → correc**tion**   (2) observe → _____
>
> (3) conserve → _____   (4) indicate → _____
>
> (5) celebrate → _____   (6) connect → _____

■ Phrase Drill

Select a proper phrase listed to complete each sentence. Changes of word forms might be necessary.

keep up with   up and down   from...to   in fashion   out of fashion

1. Green and yellow are _____ again.
2. Rita and her sister are always trying to _____ fashion.
3. Kelly's hairstyle have gone _____ now.
4. All the kids in the room jumped _____ and laughed loudly.
5. Customs differ _____ country _____ country.

Speaking task

■ Group Discussion

Discuss the following questions with your group members. Then, report your answer to the class.

1. How often does a new fashion come out?
2. What kind of clothes do you like?
3. Does fashion play an important role in your daily life? Why or why not?
4. What do you think of your parents' old clothes?

Conversation Practice

Invite a partner to practice the following conversation.

Jennifer: Hi, Cynthia! Have you read the latest fashion magazine?

Cynthia : Not yet. Any new fashions? I am going to buy some skirts.

Jennifer: Yes, you bet. This year camel skirts and A-line skirts will be fashionable.

Cynthia : Oh, no! Last year, I spent lots of money buying miniskirts.

Jennifer: You know, fashions keep changing, and you can never catch up with them.

Cynthia : You are right. By the way, remember the party on Sunday?

Jennifer: Sure! I have been thinking about what I should wear to the party these days.

Cynthia : Have you got any idea about that?

Jennifer: I probably will wear a V-neck sweater and a short skirt. And I think I will wear high boots. Besides, I will bring a handbag with me. And you?

Cynthia : I think I will wear a shirt, a miniskirt, and half boots. My mom will lend me her old shirt. I always thought it's old-fashioned, but now it's "in."

Jennifer: That's smart. You know, clothes that are in fashion this season may be out of fashion next season. Keeping up with the fashions can be very expensive. So one way to save money is wearing your parents' old clothes.

Cynthia : That's right!

▬ Questionnaire ▬

This survey is aimed at understanding how many students are aware of fashions. Interview a classmate and fill out the form.

1. Sex: _____ (Male or Female)

2. Age: _____

3. Career: _____

4. Marital status: _____ (Single or Married)

5. Where do you usually get information about fashions?
   ☐ On TV.   ☐ Magazines/Newspapers.   ☐ Friends.
   ☐ On the Internet.   ☐ Others: _____

6. How often do you go to a fashion show?
   ☐ Once a week.   ☐ Seldom.   ☐ Never.

7. How much do you usually spend on clothing each season?
   ☐ NT$10,000   ☐ NT$5,000   ☐ NT$2,000   ☐ Other: _____

8. What do you care more in choosing clothing?
   ☐ Color.   ☐ Fashion.   ☐ Material.   ☐ Your own style.
   ☐ Others: _____

9. When do you buy new clothes?
   ☐ At the beginning of the season.   ☐ When clothes are on sale.
   ☐ Only when you need some.   ☐ Others: _____

10. What dose the word "fashion" mean to you?
    ☐ Expensive.   ☐ Beautiful.   ☐ Unique.   ☐ Stylish.   ☐ Life.
    ☐ Others: _____

11. What's the most important fashion accessory to you?
    ☐ Bag.   ☐ Belt.   ☐ Glasses.   ☐ Scarf.   ☐ Necklace.   ☐ Earrings.
    ☐ Watch.   ☐ Cell phone.   ☐ Cap.   ☐ Ring.   ☐ Bracelet.   ☐ Shoes.
    ☐ Others: _____

Listening task

Part A

If the sentence you hear on the CD means the same as the sentence you read below, put "S" in the blank; if not, put "D" in the blank.

_____ 1. Wearing a skirt twenty centimeters below the knees becomes fashionable.

_____ 2. Keeping up with the fashions can be very expensive.

_____ 3. If you wait long enough, the clothes that are out of fashion today will be back in fashion someday.

_____ 4. Your mother's skirts, which you thought were very conservative, can suddenly become very stylish one day.

_____ 5. Don't throw your old clothes away. It's one of the best ways to save money.

Part B

You will hear five statements on the CD. Each statement is followed by a question. According to what you hear, select the best answer to each question.

(　　) 1. (A) It's disgusting.　　　　　　(B) It doesn't suit her.
　　　　(C) It's the "in" color this season. (D) It's out of fashion.

(　　) 2. (A) Fashions will change.　　　(B) Fashions will change people.
　　　　(C) People will change their style. (D) Shops change the fashions.

(　　) 3. (A) Find a part-time job.　　　(B) Sell your fashions.
　　　　(C) Read fashion magazine.　　(D) Keep your old clothes.

(　　) 4. (A) Pink.　　　(B) Yellow.　　(C) Black.　　(D) Gray.

(　　) 5. (A) It was fashionable at that time.
　　　　(B) The weather was hot at that time.
　　　　(C) It was very expensive at that time.
　　　　(D) The length of the skirts were unacceptable at that time.

Sentence Patterns

Use the given structure to translate each of the following into English.

If...., ...will....

Examples:

1. If you wait long enough, you will see who is telling the truth.

2. If you become a rich man, you will be able to afford this car.

Exercises:

Translate the following Chinese sentences into English ones.

1. 如果你努力工作，你會增加寶貴的經驗。

2. 如果這本書很有趣的話，我會買它。

3. 如果Jack跟我說實話，我會原諒他。

4. 如果Blair會去這個派對，我會跟她去。

5. 如果Leo準時到那裡，他會看到他最喜愛的歌手。

6. 如果Emma知道這個秘密，她會告訴我。

■ Error Correction

Look at the passage below. There are six marked words or phrases. If the marked word or phrase is correct, put "C" in the blank. If not, put correct form in the blank.

Men <u>had</u> similar problems with their shirts. Some years, it is <u>fashion</u> to wear
   (A)   (B)

a shirt with a very small <u>collars</u>. Another year, small collars become
                              (C)

<u>outdated</u> and large button-down collars are trendy. Sometimes it even
  (D)

becomes fashionable to wear shirts <u>in</u> no collars at all. A shirt that you
                                       (E)

once <u>think</u> was very trendy can look old-fashioned in a few years.
    (F)

(A) _____   (B) _____   (C) _____

(D) _____   (E) _____   (F) _____

■ Translation

Translate each of the following Chinese sentences into English.

1. 皮褲現在不流行了。

   Leather pants are _____ of _____ now.

2. 這些裙子有相似的顏色和材料。

   The skirts are _____ colors and materials.

3. 那些你總是認為太保守或者是太傳統的衣服可能會忽然變的很流行。

   The clothes which you always thought were very _____ and _____ can suddenly become very popular.

4. Lily喜歡穿寬鬆的衣服。

   Lily loves to wear _____ clothes.

5. Tom一把抓住John的領子。

   Tom seized John _____ the _____ .

■ Paragraph Writing

According to the question below, write a paragraph of 100 words in length to give your opinions about fashion.

Which one is more important? Fashion or personal style?

Acknowledgments

Body Decoration

From Body Language-Codes and Ciphers-Communicating by Signs, Writing and Numbers. Published by Wayland (Publishers) Ltd. Reprinted by permission of the publisher.

Good Luck, Bad Luck

From Project Achievement: Reading B. © 1982 by Scholastic Inc. Reprinted by permission of Scholastic Inc.

Language in Clothes

From Body Language-Codes and Ciphers-Communicating by Signs, Writing and Numbers. Published by Wayland (Publishers) Ltd. Reprinted by permission of the publisher.

Animal Communication

From Body Language-Codes and Ciphers-Communicating by Signs, Writing and Numbers. Published by Wayland (Publishers) Ltd. Reprinted by permission of the publisher.

Take a Walk

From Project Achievement: Reading D. © 1984 by Scholastic Inc. Reprinted by permission of Scholastic Inc.

Accepting Compliments

From Communicator I by MOLINSKY/BLISS, © 1994. Reprinted by permission of Prentice-Hall, Inc., Upper Saddle River, NJ.

Photo Credits

All pictures in this publication are authorized for use by: ShutterStock.

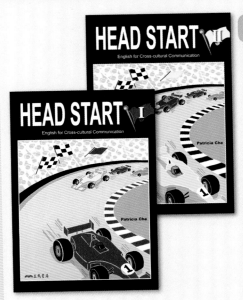